FOX AND SQUIRREL HELP OUT

Ruth Ohi

North Winds Press
An Imprint of Scholastic Canada Ltd.

For Kaarel

www.scholastic.ca

Library and Archives Canada Cataloguing in Publication

Ohi, Ruth, author, illustrator
    Fox and Squirrel help out / [written and illustrated by Ruth Ohi.]

Published simultaneously in softcover by Scholastic Canada Ltd.
ISBN 978-1-4431-6320-0 (hardcover)

    I. Title.

PS8579.H47F693 2018   jC813'.6   C2018-900097-X

Author photo by Annie T.

5 4 3 2 1   Printed in Malaysia 108   18 19 20 21 22

One day, something landed
on Fox's head.

PLOP!

"There is something on your head!"
said Squirrel.

"What?!" said Fox.
"What is on my head?!"

"Something loud," said Squirrel.
"And squeaky. But mostly loud!"

SQUEAK! SQUEAK! SQUE

3

SQUEAK! SQUEAK! SQUEAK!

The squeaky thing stayed on
Fox's head.

"Ooooooh," said Fox. "Squeak is
so soft . . .

. . . and warm."

SQUEAK!

"And loud,"
said Squirrel.

5

SQUEAK?

"Maybe Squeak is hungry," said Fox.

So Squirrel found food for Squeak.

But Squeak did not want Squirrel's food.

"Humph," said Squirrel.

"Maybe Squeak is bored,"
said Fox.

SQUEAK!
SQUEAK!

"How can Squeak be bored?" said Squirrel. "I am so exciting!"

SQUEAK!

"Look," said Fox.
"Squeak likes when
I rock back and forth,
back and forth . . .

. . . while standing on one foot!"

"Humph," said Squirrel.

"And hop like a rabbit!" said Fox.

"BUT YOU ARE NOT A RABBIT!"
said Squirrel.

"I do not think Squeak knows that," said Fox.

"Let us run and jump and play together,"
said Squirrel.

"Not now," said Fox.
"I think Squeak
needs a nap."

pant
pant

"Well, I am an excellent napper,"
said Squirrel.

But Squirrel did not nap.

And neither did
Squeak.

Hop!

18

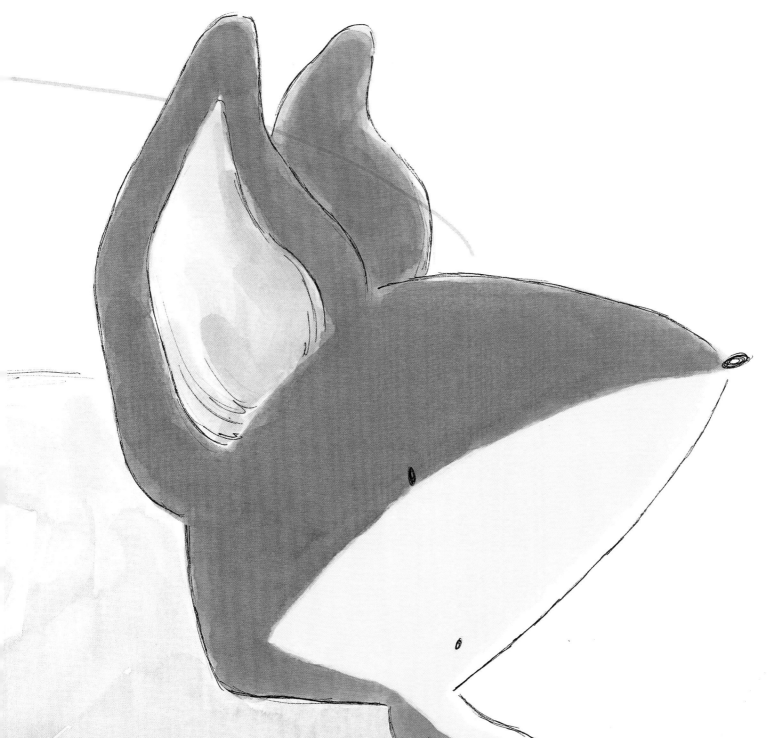

19

plop!

"Oooooh," said Squirrel.
"Squeak is so soft . . .

20

. . . and warm."

21

SQUEAK!

23

"Who is that?"

24

SQUEAK!

SQUEAK!
SQUEAK!

28

"Squeak looked happy,"
said Fox.

"Bye-bye, Squeak," said Squirrel.
"You will be missed."